ALTERNATOR
BOOKS™

CRYPTOLOGY
CLASSIC CODES
AND CIPHERS

RACHAEL L. THOMAS

Lerner Publications ◆ Minneapolis

Lerner Publications Company
An imprint of Lerner Publishing Group, Inc.
241 First Avenue North
Minneapolis, MN 55401 USA

For reading levels and more information, look up this title at www.lernerbooks.com.

Main body text set in Aptifer Sans LT Pro
Typeface provided by Linotype

The images in this book are used with the permission of: © mountainpix/Shutterstock Images, pp. 3, 10; © ilbusca/Getty Images, pp. 4–5; © Anatolii Mazhora/Shutterstock Images, p. 6; © andresr/Getty Images, p. 7; © Royal Geographical Society/Getty Images, pp. 8–9; © DEA/G. DAGLI ORTI/Getty Images, p. 11; © ZKH/Shutterstock Images, p. 12; © Hulton Archive/Getty Images, p. 13; © Bettmann/Getty Images, p. 14; © Lerner Vadim/Shutterstock Images, p. 15; © Laborant/Shutterstock Images, pp. 16–17; © Rischgitz/Getty Images, p. 18; © Grafissimo/Getty Images, p. 19; © Everett Collection/Shutterstock Images, pp. 20, 25; © UniversalImagesGroup/Getty Images, p. 21; © Encyclopaedia Britannica/Getty Images, p. 22; © Razvy/Shutterstock Images, p. 23; © mark higgins/Shutterstock Images, p. 26; © Heritage Images/Getty Images, p. 27; © gorodenkoff/Getty Images, p. 28; © Mighty Media, Inc., p. 29 (all).

Cover Photo: © National Security Agency

Design Elements: © AF-studio/Getty Images; © 4khz/Getty Images; © non-exclusive/Getty Images

Library of Congress Cataloging-in-Publication Data

Names: Thomas, Rachael L., author.
Title: Classic codes and ciphers / Rachael L. Thomas.
Description: Minneapolis : Lerner Publications, [2022] | Series: Cryptology (alternator books) | Includes
    bibliographical references and index. | Audience: Ages 8–12 | Audience: Grades 4–6 | Summary:
    "Cryptology is the art and science of secret communication, and its purpose is to protect precious
    information and keep people safe. Learn about its building blocks: ciphers, codes, and keys"—
    Provided by publisher.
Identifiers: LCCN 2020019944 (print) | LCCN 2020019945 (ebook) | ISBN 9781728404615 (lib. bdg.) |
    ISBN 9781728417950 (eb pdf)
Subjects: LCSH: Cryptography—Juvenile literature. | Ciphers—Juvenile literature.
Classification: LCC Z103.3 .T47 2021 (print) | LCC Z103.3 (ebook) | DDC 652/.8—dc23

LC record available at https://lccn.loc.gov/2020019944
LC ebook record available at https://lccn.loc.gov/2020019945

Manufactured in the United States of America
1-48519-49033-12/14/2020

TABLE OF CONTENTS

Introduction 4

Chapter 1 What Is Cryptology? 6

Chapter 2 Ancient Cryptology 10

Chapter 3 Secrets and Rivalry 16

Chapter 4 Codes, Ciphers, and War 22

Conclusion 28

Crack It! Make a Spartan Scytale 29

Glossary 30

Learn More 31

Index 32

INTRODUCTION

It was 1586, and cryptologist Thomas Phelippes was hard at work studying coded letters. The letters had been stolen from Mary, Queen of Scots. Mary had been held prisoner by her cousin, Queen Elizabeth I, for 19 years.

Phelippes pondered the strange symbols covering the parchment, looking for patterns. Some symbols appeared more often than others. And there were far more symbols than there were letters in the alphabet. Phelippes suspected that some symbols stood for words or phrases.

Phelippes used a special cryptology technique to crack the coded letters. What he found was shocking. The letters revealed plans to invade England and overthrow the queen! Phelippes rushed to inform Queen Elizabeth of Mary's plans, changing the course of history as he did.

Queen Elizabeth I

Mary, Queen of Scots

WHAT IS CRYPTOLOGY?

Cryptology is the science of secret communication. For thousands of years, soldiers, prisoners, diplomats, and more have used cryptology to protect important information.

Cryptology can be divided into two parts: cryptography and cryptanalysis. Cryptography is the practice of encoding or enciphering a message so that its meaning is hidden. Cryptanalysis is the practice of decoding or deciphering the hidden meaning of a message.

The art of cryptology has grown and developed over time. As cryptologists create stronger codes and ciphers, others rise to the challenge of cracking them! New technology has made cryptology even more complex. But no matter what, cryptology's goal remains protecting precious information.

The word *cryptology* comes from the Greek word *kryptos*, which means "secret" or "hidden."

Modern cryptology is used to protect credit card information, computer passwords, and more.

BAND : SOUTH COL UNTENAB[LE]

BOURDILLON : LHOTSE FACE IMPOSSIB[LE]

EVANS : RIDGE CAMP UNTENAB[LE]

GREGORY : WITHDRAWAL TO WEST

HILLARY : ADVANCE BASE ABANDO[NED]

HUNT : CAMP FIVE ABANDONE[D]

LOWE : CAMP SIX ABANDONED

NOYCE : CAMP SEVEN ~~ABANDON~~

TENSING : AWAITING IMPROVEMENT

WARD : FURTHER NEWS FOLLOWS
~~AWAITING REDUCED WIND~~

WESTMACOTT : ASSAULT POSTPONED

WYLIE : ~~ATTEMPT DELAYED~~ WEATH[ER]

SHERPA ; AWAITING OXYGEN SUPPL[Y]

thus : SNOW CONDITIONS BAD CAMP [FIVE]
AWAITING IMPROVEMENT

TODAY
mean : SUMMIT REACHED ∧ BY HUNT AN[D]

SNOW CONDITIONS BAD CAMPS

CIPHERS, CODES, AND KEYS

Ciphers, codes, and keys are the building blocks of cryptology. Ciphers change individual letters to make words unreadable. In a cipher, the word "animal" could become "cpkocn" or "gcengx."

A code affects entire words or phrases. For example, aircraft pilots sometimes say the code words "Roger that." This means "information received."

A cryptographer's work is challenging. A code or cipher must be complex, or it will be cracked. But it must also be possible for allies to easily decrypt. So, cryptologists create keys to help translate specific codes or ciphers.

A key can take many forms. Some are books. Others are special gadgets! No matter what form they take, keys are used to decode the hidden meaning of a message.

In 1953, humans completed the first successful ascent of Mount Everest. A reporter on the expedition used a code (*pictured*) to keep the news from leaking. The phrase "snow conditions bad" meant "summit reached."

E

E

BASIN

ED

DETERIORA

ES

TO

E ABANDONE

TENSING

X AND

ANCIENT CRYPTOLOGY

Humans have practiced cryptology since ancient times. The first known example of encrypted text is from ancient Mesopotamia. The text dates to 1500 BCE. It was written on a clay tablet in a script called cuneiform.

The message's author was an artist. This ancient cryptographer used a substitution cipher to hide a recipe for pottery glaze! In this type of cipher, one letter of an alphabet is exchanged for another. So, the ciphered recipe was muddled and impossible to understand.

Ancient glazes were made using crushed quartz mixed with blue or green minerals.

STEAM Spotlight—Art

Mesopotamia was home to the Sumer civilization. Ancient Sumerians wrote out cuneiform glyphs by etching wedge-shaped lines into soft clay. Baking a clay tablet made the material harden. This preserved important writing for others to read.

This Sumerian clay tablet shows administrative records.

Around 700 BCE, cryptographers in the Greek city-state of Sparta pioneered a new cryptographic device. The scytale is the earliest known example of an instrument designed to encipher and decipher secret messages.

The scytale was a small wooden rod. Messengers wound a strip of parchment or leather around the rod, covering its length, and then wrote notes along the strip. When unwound, the strip would show a jumble of letters. But if the strip were wrapped around the length of another scytale, the rows of letters would reveal the intended message.

Scytales were typically used to send messages across battlefields. The message sender and the message recipient had to have scytales of the exact same size and shape. This ensured that the message was spelled out correctly.

A Spartan soldier could wear a scytale message strip as a belt to conceal its real purpose.

A professor enciphers the message "attack at dawn" using a simple substitution cipher.

A document written in Hebrew, the language of the Old Testament Bible

The Atbash cipher is a cipher system from ancient Israel. Scribes of the Jewish faith used the cipher to embed secret messages into the Old Testament Bible between 600 and 500 BCE.

The Atbash cipher is a substitution cipher that reverses the order of an alphabet. The Roman alphabet, for example, begins with *a* and ends with *z*. Using the Atbash cipher, *a*'s would be replaced with *z*'s in a written message. The letter *b* would be replaced with *y*, and so on.

At the time, Jewish people often faced religious persecution. Some historians believe Atbash ciphers may have helped hide forbidden conversations. Others believe that the cipher was simply a unique writing style. Today, the purpose of the encryptions is still a mystery.

SECRETS AND RIVALRY

Cryptology has always been an important tool to conceal information during times of war or persecution. But in the Middle Ages, its role changed. Countries began using cryptology to protect everyday diplomatic relations with other nations.

Around 1200, the territories of central Italy were competing for power and influence. The princes ruling these territories developed private code and cipher systems. These systems let the princes communicate safely with one another and with other countries.

Medieval cryptologists also began building syllabaries. These were official lists of symbols and code words used to represent letters and syllables. Cryptologists consulted a syllabary to create cryptograms, or hidden messages. The syllabaries of medieval Europe would strongly influence cipher systems of the future.

A cryptogram can be made using a code, a cipher, or a combination of both.

When Mary, Queen of Scots, was being held captive in 1586, she exchanged letters with a friend, Anthony Babington. Babington wished for Mary to escape and rule England. He and Mary planned the plot in their letters.

The letters were encrypted using what is now called the Babington code. The code used symbols to represent letters. Several words and short phrases were also encoded using symbols.

Phelippes used frequency analysis to crack the Babington code. Frequency analysis is a common technique in cryptanalysis. Cryptanalysts spot patterns in enciphered text using statistics. In this way, cryptanalysts can identify common letters and words that help break the encryption!

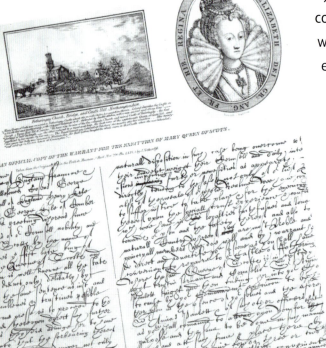

In February 1587, Queen Elizabeth I issued a warrant sentencing Mary, Queen of Scots, to death.

CRYPTO SPOTLIGHT

Frequency analysis was first introduced in 841 CE by Arab philosopher al-Kindi. He discussed the technique in his book *A Manuscript on Deciphering Cryptographic Messages*. This book is the oldest surviving work on cryptology.

Many of al-Kindi's philosophical works were influenced by the Greek philosopher Aristotle (*pictured*).

King Louis XIV

King Louis XIV ruled France from 1661 to 1715. During his reign, he invested much money in cryptology. King Louis's chief cryptographer was Antoine Rossignol. Rossignol and his son, Bonaventure, worked together to build an unbreakable cipher system for the king.

The cipher was written using numbers. Each number corresponded to a syllable in the French language. The Rossignols also added traps to the cipher. One number wasn't a syllable at all. Instead, it deleted the number before it!

The king wrote many confidential letters using the cipher. It remained uncracked during his lifetime. In 1890, military cryptanalyst Étienne Bazeries counted 587 different number combinations in the ciphered letters! Bazeries then worked for more than three years to finally crack the cipher.

Rossignol (*pictured*) and Bonaventure's cipher became known as the "Great Cipher."

CHAPTER 4

CODES, CIPHERS, AND WAR

By the 1800s, cryptography and cryptanalysis were considered essential for secure, long distance communication. This was especially important during times of war.

Around 1470, Italian architect Leon Battista Alberti had invented a cipher system called polyalphabetic substitution. Polyalphabetic substitution continually switches ciphers within a message. This cipher system works as part of a circular device called a cipher disk.

A cipher disk

Leon Battista Alberti

Four hundred years later, Confederate Army officers used cipher disks during the American Civil War (1861–1865). The brass disks made encrypting and decrypting messages fast and secure.

A cipher disk had a rotating inner wheel and outer wheel. To use a cipher disk, army leaders decided on a key word, such as *lion*. To send the message *hello*, an officer would line up the disk's outer *a* with the first letter of the key word, *l*. With these settings, the *h* of *hello* would line up with the inner *s*. So, *s* would be the first letter of the enciphered message.

The officer would then repeat these steps, using *i*, *o*, *n*, and *l* to encipher e, *l*, *l*, and *o*. The constantly shifting disk settings made messages much harder to crack.

STEAM Spotlight—Technology

By the late 1800s, the United States was entering a period of industrialization. Businesses across the country were developing machines to create products quickly and cheaply. This enabled products like cipher disks to be mass-produced.

American troops also used cipher disks to encrypt and decrypt messages during the Spanish-American War (1898).

As technology progressed, so did cryptographic devices. In 1939, World War II (1939–1945) broke out across Europe. Warring nations developed code and cipher systems to secretly communicate with allies. Germany's cipher system was called Enigma.

Enigma cipher text was generated using an Enigma machine. The machine included several rotating disks called scramblers. The scramblers created a polyalphabetic substitution cipher.

Cipher disks used during the American Civil War had two rotating wheels. But Enigma machines used up to five! The wheels rotated to encrypt each letter of a message using a different cipher. It became almost impossible to spot patterns in Enigma cipher text.

Enigma machines were battery-powered and portable.

CRYPTO SPOTLIGHT

Alan Turing was a British cryptologist who helped crack Enigma cipher text. Turing developed an electromechanical device called a bombe. The bombe could detect the scrambler settings of Enigma machines. This invention eventually led Turing's team to crack the cipher.

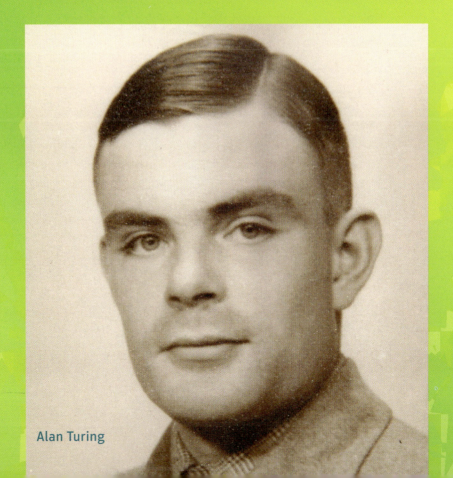

Alan Turing

Many modern cryptologists work to protect information for governments and large companies.

CONCLUSION

In the twenty-first century, cryptology is mostly digital. The systems in place to encrypt digital information rely on complex mathematics. But the rules behind these digital cipher systems are adapted from history's cryptology.

In the future, cryptology will continue to evolve. But classic codes and ciphers will ensure that our information stays safe.

Crack It! Make a Spartan Scytale

Materials
two identical pencils
sheet of paper
glue stick
scissors
clear tape
pen

1. Cut three 1/2-inch- (1.3-cm-) wide strips of paper.

2. Glue the ends of the strips together to make one long strip.

3. When dry, wind the long strip around one pencil's length.

4. Tape the end of the strip in place.

5. Write a message along the strip.

6. Unwind the strip of paper. This is your secret message!

7. Have your friend wind the strip around the other pencil's length to read the message.

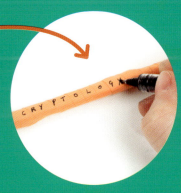

GLOSSARY

confidential: private or secret

decipher: to reveal the meaning of a ciphered message

decode: to reveal the meaning of a coded message

decrypt: to find a message's hidden meaning

diplomat: a person trained to negotiate between different nations. Something relating to the work of negotiating between different nations is diplomatic.

encipher: to hide the meaning of a message using a cipher. A message hidden using a cipher is enciphered.

encode: to hide the meaning of a message using a code

encrypt: to alter a message to hide its meaning. Once encrypted, a hidden message is called an encryption.

glyph: a symbol that communicates information

industrialization: the development of businesses and factories in a region or country

key: the tool or resource that helps a person decode or decipher a hidden message

plot: a secret plan to do something

recipient: someone who receives something

statistics: a type of mathematics that deals with the collection and analysis of data

LEARN MORE

Burrows, Terry. *Codes, Ciphers, and Cartography: Math Goes to War*. Minneapolis: Lerner Publications, 2018.

Meyer, Susan. *The History of Cryptography*. New York: Rosen, 2017.

Moore, Gareth. *Codebreaking Activity Adventure*. Washington, DC: National Geographic, 2019.

National Geographic Kids: Crack the Code
https://kids.nationalgeographic.com/games/action-and
-adventure/crack-the-code/

NSA: National Cryptologic Museum
https://www.nsa.gov/about/cryptologic-heritage/museum
/exhibits/

The National Archives: Secrets & Spies—Codes and Ciphers
https://www.nationalarchives.gov.uk/spies/ciphers
/default.htm

INDEX

Alberti, Leon Battista, 22–23
al-Kindi, 19
American Civil War, 24
Aristotle, 19
Atbash cipher, 15

Babington, Anthony, 18
Babington code, 18
Bazeries, Étienne, 21
bombe, 27

cipher disks, 22, 24, 26
cryptanalysis, 6, 18, 21–22
cryptography, 6, 9–10, 12, 19,
    21–22, 26
cuneiform, 10

digital cryptology, 7, 28

Elizabeth I (queen), 4, 18
England, 4, 18
Enigma, 26–27

France, 21
frequency analysis, 18–19

Germany, 26

Israel, 15
Italy, 16, 22

keys, 9, 24

Louis XIV (king), 20–21

Make a Spartan Scytale project,
    29
*Manuscript on Deciphering
    Cryptographic Messages, A*, 19
Mary, Queen of Scots, 4–5, 18
Mesopotamia, 10
Mount Everest, 9

Phelippes, Thomas, 4, 18

Rossignol, Antoine, 21
Rossignol, Bonaventure, 21
Rossignol cipher, 21

scytales, 12–13, 29
Spanish-American War, 25
Sparta, Greece, 12–13, 29
substitution ciphers, 10, 14–15,
    22, 26
syllabaries, 16

Turing, Alan, 27

United States, 24, 26

World War II, 26